THE WAY THINGS ARE
OR
COULD BE

Myrtle Stedman

SUNSTONE
PRESS

SANTA FE

Sunstone books may be purchased for edcational, business, or sales promotional use. For information please write: Special Markets Department, Sunstone Press, P.O. Box 2321, Santa Fe, New Mexico 87504-2321.

First Edition

Printed and bound in the United States of America

Library of Congress Cataloging in Publication Data:

Stedman, Myrtle.
    The way things are or could be/Myrtle Stedman
       p. cm.
    ISBN: 0-86534-255-5
    I. Title.
PS3569. T33823W39   1996
811' .54—dc20   96-19959
                         CIP

Published by SUNSTONE PRESS
                Post Office Box 2321
                Santa Fe, NM 87504-2321 / USA
                (505) 988-4418 / orders only (800) 243-5644
                FAX (505) 988-1025

CONTENTS

PART I: BIOGRAPHY OF THE MIND

PART II: A NEW SPRING

PART III: MOVING ON

PART IV: WITH OPEN ARMS TO THE FUTURE

PART I:
BIOGRAPHY OF THE MIND

MIND OVERLOOKED

In 1947 I wrote:
"I longed to know the Mind
and I knew it
and it knew
me—

The whole universe seemed
moved by my longing,

And I saw that the oneness
of mind
and all of its forms
is based on a love
common to
all."

Einstein is quoted as saying, "The most important thing left to be discovered is the answer to the question: Is the universe friendly?"

If all of its forms are based on a love common to all, how can we say otherwise? Or should we ask, "Is the whole universe of a biological Mind? And what can that mean?"

Some years ago I saw a TV program on *The Age Of Man*. At the end the commentator said that we still don't know how life began— he said when we do know, it will be so simple that we will wonder how we missed it.

What could have been so obvious as to have been missed but the Mind, and what could have produced biological life but, that which in itself is biological—two aspects of logic in a give and take attitude, or spirit.

Without the appearance of being male and female the mind is that, in being expressive and receptive or possibly as a description Einstein gave to two interacting waves continuing from what he called the Big Bang. His followers have not been able to see these waves visually except in their imagination projected on a computer screen.

I would like to quote more of this poem I wrote in 1947 where
I see this interaction culminating in an explosive declaration or big
bang, if you will.

"Imagine if you can
an infinite death-like
before time
rest—

Virgin Mind in semiconscious
repose.

Close your eyes
and all is

Darkness as far
as you can
see.

Watch for there is a
quickening and
a flickering of
light to be
observed—

But look, for the darkness
quickens again—

And again in a chain
until it becomes a
necessity

For the light to possess her
and she him.

And where she draws him
she also follows;

So that there is a breathing
increasing until it
mounts into an
agonizing stillness.

Then there is a blinding
flash and an ex-
plosive declaration
in the giving-and-
taking—

And when there is again
a period of rest—

There is light and darkness
divided yet
one.

And the darkness is
pregnant
with
form."

Except for the
darkness of mind
longing for the light
of mind,

There would be
no beings visible
in form,

Nor any tangible
ideas separated
from the intangible.

All space is spaced
and placed with
forms of light and
darkness.

All forms are sensitive
and all are consciously
motivated—

So that there is a
prevailing spirit—

In Genesis, we read—

"Let us make man
in our image—

Male and Female
made he them."

"Our" refers to the
expressive nature
of the Mind

And to the receptive
nature of the
Mind.

The intent or longing
expresses itself

And has no further
creative power
than that.

The reception of this intent
takes it and orchestrates
the outcome

And nurtures it
until it can take
care of itself.

Everywhere
this male and
female action of the
Mind is taking place.

"He" is electro,
"She" is magnetic,

"He" is light,
"She" is darkness,

"They" are all of the
opposites

Which can not be one
without the
other.

They together are the
"unified field" or God,

In which "we live and
breathe and
have our being."

This is the basic truth
or reality to be found

In the transcendental
experiencing of the
Mind's makeup.

It is a truth which
cannot be reduced
to singularity, except
in unity.

All being, all existence
depends on the
biological nature
of the Mind.

The Spiritual connotation
arises out of the
Mind's interaction
between the two
components of

Itself in unity of intent
to make something
of itself,

Or as we say to express
one's self.

In this I see the virgin darkness of the Mind as the womb from which all things are born, animate or inanimate. Long ago I read this and I am not going to tell you where it was written because half of you will discount it before I begin and the other half will say, "That is not the way I heard it." I would like you to listen as though you never heard it before. Don't miss a thing:

"In the beginning was the Word and the Word was with God, and the Word was God. The same was in the beginning with God. All things were made by him, and without him was not anything made that was made. In him was life; and the life was the light of men. And the light shineth in the darkness and the darkness comprehended it not." (St. John 1, 1-5 if you really want to know.)

Quote again from my 1947 poem:

> And it should not be said
> anymore—
> "and the darkness
> comprehended it
> not."
>
> The darkness is the
> receptive side
> of the
> Mind—
>
> A virgin field of openness, the
> female reciprocal—
>
> Willingness to be and
> let there
> be
>
> Multitudinous forms
> of the Mind.

If we like what we are we will not resent any part of the biography of the mind which has brought us to this conclusion. We will see the differing cultures and customs for what they are or were without brainwashing, but as important leads to a universal simplicity basic to all our complexities and take a real look—a cleansing look at a love common to all in a totally virgin or—nothing but look at life.

In this day and age has anyone suspected, let alone agreed, that the two words biological and spiritual have the same meaning or, if they should, what this could do to our world view?

Myrtle Stedman

TO THE READER

Years ago my husband
told me

"You can't change
the world."

But it was he who
declared—

"Most of what we
call love

Is simply a biological
urge."

And he went on to
say—

"Nature made it
pleasant
in order to maintain
the species."

At first I was hurt.

Then it became my
inspiration—
my drive

To put this into its
proper
juxtaposition

I did what all women
do who are
in love—

I put all reasoning
out of the
way.

And just looked
at the way
things are

Or could be.

THIS IS A DAY OF DISRESPECT

IMBALANCES

This is a day of disgruntled
dis-respect

Toward God, man
for anything or
anybody
that gets
in our
way.

We pollute the air
and pollute
the land and
sea.

It is a wonder
that the planet
doesn't

Shiver and shake
us all out
into space.

There are hurts
and imbalances
where we
would

Least suspect—
in the home
and in the church,

Fathers molesting
their daughters
or badgering
their
sons,

Priests with starved
and misguided
biological
urges

Sexually abusing
children,

Homes are bombed
and churches
burned.

Is this telling us
anything?

WHAT NEXT

Will the ones
doing the
shooting

In a starving
country

Turn cannibalistic
and eat
their hunt?

Perish the thought!

Or let it be.

MEN IN HIGH PLACES

Men in high places
or in low
for that
matter

Who use their
biological
urge

As a play thing
are finding
themselves
in
trouble—

Women are more
openly
revealing
themselves

Inviting play
or independently
making a
statement

Against it—

And for the real
thing.

DON'T INHIBIT YOUR CHILDREN

Rational belief
had us believing
fifty years
ago

That when it comes
to the art of
living,

"Don't inhibit your
children."

It did make for
confidence
and
poise

And for truly
vital children.

"Let them watch and
hear of violence
too," it was
said—

Because they could
in that or through
that way experience
and learn

From emotions
without themselves
being
involved.

I almost slammed
my kitchen door
off its hinges
in protest,

But it did no
good—

That long
ago.

Now children
are having
children—

Carrying guns to school
and shooting
their parents—

And grandparents.

CRUELTY WITHOUT THINKING

Family members
can be more
cruel than
anyone
else.

Because they are
family members
they think it
their right—

To put other family
members in the
way they
think.

Which is not
thinking—

Not thinking
of the other
person's
rights—

To think for
themselves.

But maybe thinking
is not the
ultimate goal.

AND MOTHER'S DAY

Some will ask—
"What do you mean
Mother's day—

A day to swish the
just born
down the
john,

Or stuff it in the
garbage
can?"

There are some
mothers who
think nothing

Of eating their young.

Then again I know
a guy who
hasn't spoken
to his
mother

For sixteen years.

Maybe she didn't
want him
in the first
place.

There are ugly seals
that weigh a ton
that tromp on little ones

In the heat
of making
more
of their brats.

I can't or don't want
to remember
his name.

And in the war
now going on,
and again, I can't
remember the
name of
the place,

Neighbors are made
to mate with
neighbors

Though enemies now;
with the idea of this
mix to make
a more
uncemented fare.

This is what we need
though harsh
in the making.

My sons
I am glad you
were born
in the day you
were born,

I wanted both
of you.

And not only I
but your father
too.

This is not to say
there are not a lot
of fathers and mothers
like us
today.

There are more
than ever
before,

In spite of what
I had earlier
to say.

HAPPINESS

Becoming happy
in the morning
when one wakes up

Is not like
getting up
and sprinkling
sugar

On one's breakfast food
or pushing a button
on the radio.

It takes more
than
that.

The only real
happiness
on the
shows

These days

Are the ads
that come
in between.

There, husbands
and wives
and children

Are all smiles
loving
and glad

To be eating a certain
brand
of oatmeal,

Or are showing
how tough
and brave
their
new trucks

Or cars are—
disregarding

Knowing they will have
to take them

To the repair shop
the next
day.

AS LIFE IS

When I was a child
there were always
grownups
whispering,

Not just behind
closed doors,

But where the one
being whispered
about

Could plainly see
the dropped facade.

None paid any
attention
to me

And I never paid
any attention
to what
they were
whispering;

Maybe that is
why children
as a rule
(especially boys)
like to play
war.

Those children of the men
who were children
when I was
a child

Are now shooting
to be done
with the mystery
in whispering;

Purging it is called.

But if the dead
never die
what then?

It is still behind
a facade.

There is a place
to begin
anew.

And that is in
the beginning.

And here
we start
with the
Mind

And with the assumption
that it was in
the beginning,

And that our own
consciousness
started
right
there.

And ask ourselves
was that good
or bad?

That is the question.

And are we a mix
or could we
choose

And be true
to one or the
other?

The ball
bounces right
back to
us.

And our only
salvation
is to make that
choice.

And if we choose
to think life
is bad,

Who cares about
salvation?

So I'll just back up
and accept
life as it
is.

And that is to say
I've made my
choice—

I see life as
good—

Even when there
appears to be
otherwise.

THE SAME MIND

How can anyone
of us think
that our views

Are so right—

When we all share
the same
Mind?

We can have a
view that
no one else

Has yet thought of,

But the minute
we do

The thought is out
there

For anyone ready
and open
to conceive

What it is that we
have seen
and
expressed,

Or even, kept to ourselves
supposedly.

IT IS NOT A QUESTION

It is not a question
of moral,
cult or
creed.

It is a lack of basic
understanding
of the interaction
of the Mind,

And of the realization
that Mind
is Mind

And not many
minds.

ONE MIND

To know that there is
one Mind
and that,
good—

It has to be good,
no?

If there were not
Mind

There would be nothing
to make
anything

And nothing to register
the fact of
non-existence,

So we almost have
to acknowledge
the fact
that

Mind is good—

Nothing bad
about it!

That is a pure and
simple
statement.

Knowing is the key word
to experiencing
its goodness.

The Mind is expressive
and receptive,

So it is conscious of
itself.

Having no other
consciousness
except of
itself

It knows
only
good.

THE MIND MULTIPLIES AND SUBTRACTS

When I express richness
I am receptive
to riches

And I will experience
a richness.

If I express lack
the Mind will
subtract

From that which
I have

And I experience
lack.

We can not express
something that
we have not already
been receptive to.

The Mind agrees
and it
agrees to
disagree.

It is good to know
what it is up to
at all times.

UNCONDITIONAL LOVE

The Mind is productive
of whatever is in
the Mind

It is the Father and Mother
all in One.

It is this "no matter
what"

That is unconditional
Love.

It is that pure
potential,

It is electro:
it is magnetic:

In one word
electromagnetic.

It is the yin
and the yang:
male and female.

It is a movement
from here to
there:

It is a going out
and a going in:

All this is why we
call it Love
or love.

All this is why we
call it Spirit
or spirit.

The word Love
or love
indicates
a Spirit
or spirit.

Love is an expression
to be conceived:

It is this excitement
that results
in birth.

When you think
of someone
your thoughts
go out
to that one:

They can not
resist it.

We have always
this going out
and going in,

Because it is the
very nature
of our
being.

It is the nature
of Being.

It is perfection
Supreme.

Imperfection
falls away
just thinking
this way.

Sickness and
disease
fall away;

Fall out of the Mind
and mind;

Fall away
from the one
you are
thinking
of,

If you are exercising
the Spirit
of Love

Or the spirit of
your love.

The word Love
embodies
Spirit

And becomes
flesh.

Rebirth
and birth
are the
same.

All is a becoming:

An expansion of thought:

Contracted
into things:
given
birth.

There is a falling
away

But nothing
is lost:

It just comes
and
goes.

It is the going
that we do not
understand,

But it has to go
in order
to come and

It takes an all out
and an all in
effort to
make a
change.

It is not the word
that does the
job,

But the spirit of
the word.

This is what is meant
when we say
we are Spiritual
beings.

The Great Spirit
is not something
apart from
us;

It is our very life,
without and
within;

It is the pro-creator
when we are young,

It is wisdom and
understanding
when we grow
old.

It is wisdom to
realize that
we give
birth

To more than
ourselves.

THE SUBSTANCE OF
BIOLOGICAL LIFE
AND OF THINGS

"In the beginning was
the Word
and the Word was
with God
and the Word was
God."
                 St. John 1:1

In its projection
there was
power—

In its acceptance
there was
conception

And consciousness
was born.

Consciousness was
born in the Mind's
reproductive
process.

All is a reproduction
of the All Powerful
thought.

That which is uppermost
in the Mind is
God,

If it finds itself
receptive
to its own
idea.

It is that the expressiveness
of the Mind has
to depend on the
receptiveness
of the Mind,

Which makes life
biological—

Two phases of the Mind
working together
as one—
with intent,

Or with spirit—
creating things
of the spirit.

GIVEN BIRTH

We are born of
the spirit
of love

Because the universe
was born of
the spirit
of love.

Some people would
say, "Divine
Love."

It is Divine
because it
is so
precious;

That is Love.
It is Divine
because it is
so overwhelming;

It is Divine
because it is
so subtle,
so small;

It is in just a
touch:
It is in a lash:

It is positive
and negative.

COMPANIONSHIP

Perfect companionship
is within the
Mind
itself;

In intercourse
between an
expression

And its acceptance;

In a touch
and a reaction;

In the peak of a wave
and its recession;

In the drawing of a breath
and its expulsion;

In the flip of a fishtail
and its propulsion,

In a sound
and a listening,

In a look in an eye
and recognition.

It is a child in a swing
and a foot on
the ground.

It is in the beat of
a heart
and a pulse
in the hand.

It is a pen in the hand
and a word
on the page.

Can you mention
anything that
does not
enjoy

Companionship;

This cause
and effect;

This openness
and filling;

This longing
and satisfaction;

This being
and not
being;

This motion between
knowing
and not knowing;

Between what one
can see
and not
see?

It is the very
nature
of the
universe

And everything
within it;

And a condition
we are never
outside of
or
without.

The urge,
not the Big Bang,
started it all
off—

And gave this
life and energy
to everything.

BE MINE

Mind be mine,
not something
out there
but not
here.

Let me not be
ignorant of
my source,

But conscious that
source and
tributary are
the same.

EARTHLY OR HEAVENLY

So let me get on
with it—
whatever it is.

This is the place
where everything
is done;

Following the design
on our own
drawing board.

Would you call this
being earthly
or being heavenly?

That is the question
of today.

It can not be less
than both.

PART II:
A NEW SPRING

UNTIL SPRING COME

Winter is still here
with three inches
of snow.

But the sun is shining
warming the air
into the breath
of Spring.

I feel this—
though I am like
the old cottonwood
tree that stands
at the edge
of the river.

My face is like
its bark;
a little wrinkled
but strong,

Showing a determination
and also a willingness
to stand like it stands
until Spring come.

DO IT AGAIN

Spring is a time
of total recall
to do it
again.

Do what again?

The sap comes up;
we bud
and bloom,

We pollinate again
in word and song
in hellos and
good-byes.

EVOLVING

We have evolved from
a single expression
"The big bang," the
scientists call it,

And what was it
that heard the
big bang,

Except that which
made it?

Did it turn around
and swallow it
whole—

Sound and echo,
male and female

And that is where
we all come
from—

Every living thing
and that which
we call non-living.

To evolve there has to be
one that makes
a noise,

A noise that has
never been heard
before;

One that freezes
that one in his tracks
—an ice age.

Is that what happened
to the dinosaurs?

I saw a cartoon once
which pictured them
in neckties and coats
sitting at desks,

While the turtle that was,
is now no more
than turtle

And a piece of joint grass
was not changed
an iota from
what it was in the
beginning.

What happened when
the hundredth monkey
learned a new trick?

Monkeys the world over
began to know that too.

So there must be a knowing
and a hearing or an
openness to that knowing

That has to do with intent.

An intent to make a
noise—

A real bang
it sounds
at first

Then it smoothes out
with time
and acceptance,

Until another big bang
is heard.

BRAINS

There are far more
brains in our head
than we use
the experts
tell us.

So why are they there
unless there is a
knowing that
knows

That we will one day
need them?

This knowledge that
there is more
to know

Is what keeps
us going.

Don't worry if you
lose a little brain tissue
when you get
older.

That knowing knows
that brains are
only the receiver.

Wait a minute—
what am I saying?

Receiving can't be less
than that which shouts,
then brains are important
don't let any
slip away—

They are the evidence
of our intent
to live,

Through pro-creation
or how?

If there were no mystery
we wouldn't try
to figure anything
out.

If there is such a thing
as all-knowing
it must be
bored to death

Or having fun
at our expense.

OPEN

I am tired of my own thinking
I don't want to read about
what others are thinking—
I am at a standstill—

Nothing going on in my head
nothing going in or going out,
resting—asleep with my eyes
open,
completely
re-laxed,

Not even waiting—
but open.

Like the sands on the shore
I know the waves will come
and rough me up
again—so what?

I'll just settle again
for more.

One of our great philosophers
was asked—or more
to the point, heard someone
say to him,

"You are so wise, you
must read a lot."

"No," he said, "if I read a
lot I would know
no more than other
men know."

That is what I am relaxed
about and open to;
a knowing that just
comes because it knows.

To this I should
not only give
a tenth of my
brain,

But do what is
admonished by
Malachi 3:10—

"Bring ye all the tithes
into the storehouse,
that there may be
meat in mine house,

And prove me now
herewith, saith
the Lord of hosts,

If I will not open
you the windows
of heaven,

THERE IS A KNOWING

And pour you out
a blessing,

That there shall
not be
room enough
to receive it."

When there is an
all-out reliance
on this mind

It co-ordinates and
harmonizes in the
best possible
ways,
all things.

There is a knowing
beyond all knowing
of where it is or
how it got there.

But there it is
when we open
a book

Or have a need
of penny
or seed;

Or of a spelling.

I am always laughing
amazed and
pleased

And praise it to the skies.

It surely seems a
presence—
but what kind
of presence
would know

Say in a book
of nine hundred
pages

To guide a finger
to open at the
exact page

And the eye to see
what we want
to see

Among thousands
of words and thousands
of books
the very word
we need
indeed!

It gives me the greatest
joy.

It is tantalizing,
frustrating,
and reassuring
all in one.

Ask the Runes
and the Tarot cards.

Or ask Elijah as he dwelt by the
brook Cherith how the ravens
brought him bread and flesh
in the morning and bread
and flesh in the evening.

He would say it is
the work of God.

And God it is
but in a depth of Mind
or in a height of Mind,

That we have as yet
not fathomed
or been able to reach
to measure or prove

That it is far or near—
separate from us
or an ability triggered
by need,

Or imagination.

ALL I NEED TO KNOW

When I go,
as it is said
when one dies,
I want to know where
I am going.

And this, I think, depends
on where I think
I am going—

If it is a smooth
continuum as life
here is—
from cause to effect,

And if all
cause is of God
and if God is the
One Mind
in all,

Then it is what
we think which
makes us in
His image
and likeness

And if anything
is eternal
it would be
the Mind,
or so we think
and are.

And about life after
death—

We won't even
have to consciously
think of what we
want to do
or be.

It would be like it is
when one opens a book
and have their eyes
see exactly the most
appropriate thing for
the occasion—
in the whole book.

This Mind knows before
we ask what it is
we need.

And this is what I need
and all I need
to know
about where I will
go when
"I go."

I will go and be
what will be
the most appropriate
for me.

And so it will be
as I think
it will be.

NURTURING INTENT

I should start this day
with praise
and thanks-
giving.

I know from experience,
exceptional as
it may be,
it is there.

What?
An intent—
an intent that belongs
to life—to live
that needs to be
nurtured.

Fear would drive it
away or dwindle
it to nothing.

I have told myself
time and again
that I can not
believe

In anything I do not
understand,

But I have experienced
this thing
—so many times,

I love it
and that is its
nurturing.

I can cry out
and hear only
an echo
or nothing
at all,

It is absolutely
impersonal,
non-judgmental
yet calmly reassuring.

What do we need
other than an
intent to
live?

There is not a spot
in our body or life
where intent cannot
touch.

IF THAT IS THE WAY
IT IS DONE BY TREE

It is nine o'clock
in the morning

I've had my second
cup of coffee
and my bath;

All I want to do
is go back
to bed.

This is a sure
indication
that I am
unconsciously
leaning toward
quitting.

But—

Every cell in my body
and every organ
agree—

After Winter
that Spring
is come.

So let me put on
my golden leaf
to let it fall
and enrich
the ground

Where all my sap
will sleep
and grow
deep

That my next spring
shall blossom
well,

And not only blossom
but bear fruit
that cell and
organ together
make

That there may be
more young
to do

As I have done
and will—

Life after life
after life.

If that is the way
it is done by
tree

Then surely this
or another
way is
for me.

NEVER FORGET

"Ask, and it shall be
given you;

Seek, and ye shall
find;"
Matthew 7:7

Let me never forget
that I have
this privilege.

WHAT WOULD IT TAKE

I heard, "This is the
solution to the
sight."

But my consciousness
became too alert
to get the message.

How can I encourage
this kind of
knowledge
to come
through?

I had been wondering
what it would take
for my eyes to
see clearly:

I was about to fall
off to sleep
when I heard
this.

It is something my
waking consciousness
can not figure
out,

And the doctor has
not been able
to bring
about.

I shall again,
and this time
ask my eyes—

"What would it take?"

Eyes are a form of
intelligence
so what

Can they themselves
divulge?

What state of consciousness
need I to be in
to hear "the solution
to the sight"?

There are no divisions
between states
of consciousness

So what keeps us
from going
from one state
to another?

If states had boundaries
they would be only
imaginary,

So let us use imagination
to break these imaginary
boundaries.

Say, there is a universal Mind,
its nature creative
having no illusionary
boundaries;

Reaching that point
of view we should
clearly see;

And there would be
my "solution
to sight."

And I would know;

There is no limit
to what the eye
can see
intellectually

And so see
all that it was
designed
to see—

Literally.

BACK TO THE DRAWING BOARD

I want to see a new
consciousness

That suits an expansion
beyond the now
physical plane,

What as it is
may be outdated
for some of us
not for all,

A passage into the
realm of
unmanifested
ideas.

Back to where we
began
to begin again

Or stay awhile
on the drawing
board.

I can't imagine
anything more
wonderful
than

What we have,

Counting the infinite
possibilities the Mind
provides us
with.

AN EVER RECURRING DREAM

I had a dream
of a nature
that keeps
returning.

I am in Sted's presence
but feel rejection

Or maybe it is something
else—

I am always walking
away but feel
his eyes on me,
conscious
of my
loneliness,

And of his own?

He had once said,
"We are soulmates
doomed to each other."

And I said, "That sounds
gloomy;" meaning
the way he said it.

But soulmates
must be something
more than physical
attraction;

More than personal
likes and dis-
likes;

More than just
rational
thinking.

It must be something
we all want,
but are afraid
that it is not
there;

It must be something
devoid of all
we think we know
of each other;

Something basic
something that
all religions
feel but
do not
know;

Something as pure
and simple
as electro-magnetics;

A love that is Love,
unconditional,
unreproving,
universally
unmoving

And stable.

But who wants such
stability for
long?

It must be a restful
reprieve

But variety and
excitement
are the spice
of our life.

Such stability
would give
us nothing
to write
about;

Nothing to tear us
apart

Or put us back
together again,

Nothing to reach for
and grow;

Just Spirit
without spirit.

How should our
soul-matedness
be expressed

Now that he is gone
and I am
here?

This is an urgent
question.
Maybe this is what
he is expressing
in these dreams
I have of him.

I do not know how
to be receptive
to what he is
expressing.

But there it is
expression and
receptivity—

These two are the
soulmates
of all that
is
and are.

It is that interacting two-way
wave the
scientists are
looking
for.

IN SPIRIT

In Spirit, as pure potential
there are no accidents
no sickness
no death,

No limits,
no barriers—

Only creative
access to
unmolded material,

Energy,
—health,
—success,

In this we can
dip
and sip

And expand
with the
universe

Objectively.

COME CLEAN

When I awoke this
morning

There was a cloud
of despair
within me.

All week it has
been there,

Like an afterbirth
of some
experience

Undispelled.

This is September.

It is Tom's birthday
today.

The day he was born
the doctor
commented,

"This baby is so clean."

And he said to my husband,
"It's because
your wife

Doesn't smoke,
doesn't drink
or take drugs."

But there must be
—I know what
it is,

That keeps haunting
me.

It is, as a man
he could never
quite leave
me,

Nor I turn loose
of him.

His death at fifty-seven
didn't change that
one bit—

He is still with me.

Oh God,
let this day be truly
his birthday,

One of joy and
thanksgiving;

Free from the womb
in which he was
conceived.

And let him come
clear and clean,

Allowing no lingering
doubt, of the
love that guides us,
to remain.

For on this same day,
maybe this very hour,

A great-grandchild
could be born
bearing his
genes,

My own,
its mother's,
her mother's,

Its father's—his father's
and all the tribes
of the earth

Carrying the mobility
of spirit supreme.

We don't have to
hold on.

Then again
why not?

It is part of the scheme.

I love to remember
how my mother
used to say,

"Don't talk with your
hands and
you don't have
to bob your
head."

And when my sister
would go out
the door,

She would say to her,
"Straighten up
that back."

And how Tom
would say,

"I can think of nothing
but to live
on this
place,"

Meaning the place
where as a boy
he grew up.

These are the things
our genes
are made
of.

And in a grandchild (his)
that desire
could easily
be realized,

This day!

Or when it is
right.

This is the way
the future
is made.

There is no reason
for despair
or to be
distraught

About anything.

The Mind is God
working His
wonders

In mysterious ways
carrying dreams
—and debris

From generation
to generation—

From yesterday to
today and
beyond

For unto us a child
is born.

But let us not
blame God if
it is debris,

I say, "fiddle sticks
to this mystery."

And let me open
my eyes

For the view that God
is my life

And that it is up
to me

What I shall
do or not
do.

ONE PERSON DOES COUNT

Still—
I wake with a feeling
as though I can't
breathe to the bottom
of my lungs;

It's a feeling of unfulfillment
in spite of my life
being full;

It's a feeling that
I need to cry
in sobs that
reach down
and into
that emptiness

To open a door to it
that I feel I have
somehow
closed—

Why do I feel that sobs
have to fill it
before there
is joy
there?

What assertion
do I have to
make
to open up
that space?

Is there some darkness
yet in my life
that I have
to explore—

Or just a bit of wisdom
that I have yet
to come upon?

And maybe it's not
just for me
but all of
us—

A pushing toward
an evolutionary
advancement.

This has long been an
era of individualism,

Me first, sort of thing—
a hero,
a leader,

One God we look up to

While this emptiness
is in the pit of the
stomachs of
the starving
and the
poor

Everywhere.

FROM THE HORSE'S MOUTH

If you long
for inspiration

It comes direct
from the
Horse's mouth.

If you read for
inspiration

It comes
indirect,

As a hand-me-down
dress
or an old
necktie.

Yet, better these
than nothing.

After all—
It is the inspiration
that
counts.

So we feel good
in the
dress

And sport
the necktie.

"—all mine are thine
and thine are
mine—"
St. John 17:10

THE ESTHETIC

Having said all
what more is
there to do?

There is a well-known
story of a man
who never saw
darkness.

He led his companions
through the desert
by night

Directing them to turn
left or go right.

And in the morning
they saw that his
feet were unscratched.

He was full of God
and this was
his ecstasy.

His whole wants
satisfied in
One.

While we with
the same
feeling

Create light bulbs,
telephones,
typewriters
and
computers,

Have running water
and beds to
sleep on,

Cars and all
sorts of things,

What is the difference?
There is none!

No difference?
No difference!

One to one
the Mind
reveals its kind

Spring after spring
after spring.

PART III:
MOVING ON

IT IS TIME TO DECIDE

It is maybe time to
decide

What to hold onto
and what to
discard;

What do I want
my genes to
convey—

And what to forget;

Have I loaded
them with
debris?

What fat am I carrying
around?

What is in my house
that hinders
and clutters

And delays its cleaning?

Am I a walking
curio shop,

Or a catalog full
of things I
don't need?

Will my expanding
consciousness
call for carrying
all this stuff;

Even, should I have
to deal with a
thousand
questions,

Or write them down,
check them off,
and throw the
list away?

It is not now spring
but it is always
time

For a clean house;

To clean up
my mind

So the best of my
expectations
can be
realized.

Like Ezekiel,
I am a rebellious
house

When it comes to
having faith

In things I do not
understand.

I'd like to think
that I might be
feeling the hurts
and injustices
toward all

The oppressed—
all the ignorance
where wisdom
should be—

To know that
the One
must
be All or

None.

So here is the beauty
of being of One
Mind;

One person does count.

So let me forget
the damage
done

By the me-first
attitude;

The leaders leading
in the wrong
way;

Forget the One God
that seems to
have forgotten
me or
doesn't show
care,

When I think
it should.

All these things are
stumbling blocks

That make me stop
and think;

If one person
could do harm
to all

One person could do
good for all,

If One God could
level houses
in a storm,

Or let one man
shoot others
in a war,
One God could stop
it all.

Let me stop having
thoughts and emotions
running wild

And realize—
one thought;

One person
does count;

In this collection
of all of One Mind
and that,
God,

And do my part.

LOOKING AT THE UNIVERSE

When we look at
the universe,
as a whole,

We have to take in
every little
dot;

That may be us—
it may be
a fly

Or another planet;

It may be a thought—

Or a whole philosophy—

Everything counts.

Every thought
and every
action

Has gotten us where
we are;

We can not go
further
without

These things being
underfoot
all the way.

So let us stop
burning,
stoning,

Crucifying, grumbling
and groaning.

Or again—

What have I said?

Nothing has happened
without
our
choosing,

Maybe not even
the worst thing
has been
bad—

If we have the
kind of civilization
we want.

The best and only
thing worth
knowing

Is that we have
the mind
to do
our choosing;

For ourselves
yes—

But what about
the whole
universe?

Mind has to be
bigger than us;

A Mind that we are
only conscious
Of in
part.

A God?
God, let it be

For without it
there would be
nothing in
charge—

That is the real meaning
of God;

Our Father in heaven—
so let it be too—

What is there except
the heavens and
everything in
it?

And how would there
be any invention
without

Something to Father it?

And a Mother Superior
why not—

To give shape and form
to everything
we want.

Do we worship these
two;

Again, why not
if we are grateful
For the way
things are?

They gave us the
only life,

The only consciousness
we have,

But wait up—
what are we
talking
about?

We are talking
about a figure
of speech;

The Word that was
in the beginning,

Which gives identity
to everything—

To us and the planets—
indicative of
the presence
of Mind.

Such as, "Let there be
light,

And there was light."

We cannot discount
anything
that is.

Or we would have
no grounds
to go
forward.

THE EXPANDING STORY

The stars and the planets
have long been
looked upon,

By wise men and
fools alike,
as the brain cells
of the universe—

As an open book
ever writing
itself;

Never quite repeating
but ever
going on.

The energy of their
knowing
radiating
outward,

Penetrating, activating,
carrying out,
encouraging—

Gathering together
the things that
we know

And spewing them out in
an expanding
story.

Spring after Spring
and more.

DREAMS

My life has proven
to me,

Dreams do come
true.

I remember very well
looking at a woodland
one particular
day

And dreaming, visualizing,
imagining,

Whatever you want to
call it;
of

A house for myself
and my family,
with trees
all about.

In the seven houses
that have been
built for
me

I've had nothing
but this
kind of place.

I remember the night
I knelt at my
window,

And prayed,
"God, keep the man
I am to marry
and bring him
to me."

"Do you love me?"
he asked.

"You are all and
more than
I asked for,"
I told him.

When I was a little girl
I always played-like,
or "plack,"
I called it.

And now that
I am old,

I am going to play-like
I have a pot
of gold.

I'll put it in the bank
and live off
the interest,

I'll take care of
my houses

And take care of
the trees,

I'll be generous
to my helpers,

And I'll write,

And I'll paint

And I'll share
all my
dreams;

While the bank
goes on and on
using

My pot of gold,
and paying
me interest

On my play-like
dream.

JEALOUSY

There were
from time to time,

Those who were
jealous of me;

It was never
quite clear
just why.

I could always
find a reason

That they should be
happy and
proud of
themselves,

But not in the beginning,
because it always
seemed such
a personal
stab;

And I would wonder,
did I do this
or did I do that?

This could go on
for years
and has.

But now I've pinned
it down
and see
it

As a round-a-bout
compliment,

And laugh with glee
and fun

And just go on
being
me—

Yet careful not to
push my
luck;

There were things I
learned on that
round-a-bout
route.

STUCK

I am stuck in a
state of consciousness,
the third
part of
the Mind.

Why can't I
reach out
to the expressive
and to the
receptive
areas

And bring something
else into that
stuck place,

That will blast it
out of its
misery?

Consciousness is not
the creator.

It is the created

With the potential for
being creative.

I am tired of what
I am thinking
about.

Is that the force (the urge)
that will bring
something else
about?

What stick do I need
to use

To get things moving
again?

What bell
do I need to
ring?

Help!

I am hung up.

Give me a
shove.

What love potion
do these two,
who are
responsible

For creation,
need
to get together?

What live thing
is waiting to
be born,

Or what invention
will they father
and mother

If they get moving?

I am waiting
impatiently
to know.

KNOWING
WITHOUT KNOWING

Fortunes have been
made and
lost

Over who thought
of what
first;

As who invented the
light bulb
or the radio.

It's the hero attitude,
the leader,
the warrior

Or the plain old
"I told you so"
thing.

We have been brought up
in a fickle
atmosphere;

One that believed
in Gods or
God

Without knowing
what God
is.

It is time that someone
solve the
mystery
for
everyone;

By quoting what someone
has said
before and

It is time for
plain
talk.

It is time to make
more
history

By saying something
simple—
Something
different!

And let it be—
Let it sink in—
Like "the Mind is biological,"
It gives birth to every-
thing

And makes everything
of its spirit, Spiritual.

AN ANTIHISTAMINE

My son,
why were you
uncomfortable
while at my
house?

What did I say
to you yesterday
or years ago

That lies in your
memory like
a weed?

What gives you
this allergy?

You removed
artificial flowers
from your
room.

"That was it,"
you said.
But was it
now?

I saw to it
that they were
clean before
you came.

I've walked in
the orchard and
picked every leaf
in my path

To hear in their
rustling an inkling
of your need.

But why look for
trouble,
your trouble is
gone.

What was your
antihistamine—

Your love for me
and mine for
you?

We both had a dose
of whatever it was—

Unbottled maybe
in a kiss and a
squeeze.

BEING AWARE

"I thank thee Father,
that thou
hearest
me."

That is the key
that unlocks
the
door

To whatever one
is praying
for;

That is the creative
principle—

Recognition
of the openness
of the
Mind

And of its readiness
to respond;

In plain English
that is just
being
aware.

Of course things
happen without
our being
aware

Because the principle
is already
set up;

It is as simple
as breathing

And automatic,
having once been
approved.

RIGHT FOR ME

"Let the words of
my mouth

And the meditations
of my heart

Be acceptable unto
thy sight,
O Lord."
(The Bible)

For that alone
is right
for me;

You are my rock
and my foundation.

THE PERFECTION OF MIND

The Mind is perfection—
we get what we ask for,
we get what we need;
this is the harmony
of the Mind.

What we ask for
is not often

A conscious act;

That is why we
disbelieve.

Real asking
and real need
are realized
only where
there is

This harmony—
in the perfection
of the

Parental creative
act;

A complete giving in
to the biological
urge,

Just to do
whatever there
is to do.

A NEW CONSCIOUSNESS

I want to see a
new consciousness—

Born of the universal
Mind;

That
Male and Female
Mind.

I want to see
each individual
as one or the
other of these
two aspects—

Or both.

Sex is rampant
among the weak
and the poor
as well as the strong
and dominant;

In and out of season
and some in confusion
male to male
and female
to female,

Having both in their
nature

Urging us to know
one another.

Only as, or until,
we know one another
will that new
consciousness
be born—

In God's own
image,
anew.

The universe is expanding
we are too—
consciously.

Let us recognize
that the Mind
is basically
Male and Female

In union one—
expressive and
receptive;

Never losing sight
of this, see
the diversity

These two create by
being of One Mind
objectively,

Ever creating a new
consciousness.

DO MORE FOR OURSELVES

"I am God, there is
none else."
(The Bible)

If I am God and there
is none else

Then I am God
through and
through.

This idea could
clear up
anything.

It could clip an
allergy

In the bud—

Could save tests,
money, doctors
and time.

I love doctors
so don't
get me
wrong—

It is just that we
could do
more

For ourselves.

MY HOME

My home is a
hallowed
spot.

I am not going
to like
not being
here

When I am
gone;

So I'll take it with me,
every inch,
every pot
and vine.

I'll store it in mind
until there is
no difference,
between me
and mine.

TO DIE IS A COP-OUT

To die is a cop-out
in every sense

For better or worse
as the case
may be.

It simply means
one needs
a change

Of life-style
with no offense
to anyone.

Why can't we give
each other
the freedom
to die—

To go in the direction
of their
desire;

Because we are
not convinced
that there
is more

To live for
and more life
to live.

There is always
consciousness
out there;

It belongs to
the Mind
in general—

It is everyone's
for the
asking,

No, we don't even
have to
ask;

It is a gift—ours
allowing
for
moving on.

THIS CHRISTMAS DAY

How big is my
universe—

No bigger than an atom—

No bigger than what
I am thinking
today?

Or does it reach
and include
all of the
stars,

Not just one?

When I pray—
Our Father
which art
in heaven—

Who is He
and what is
that heaven—

What, but the heaven
we know

And all of the stars
and more—
that we
see,

The planets
and the
one we are
on?

Hallowed be thy
name, who
envisioned such
a thing—

And keeps it all
in order!

Is not this
your Kingdom
and you, the
expressive
Mind,

Its King?

Let your Prince
of Peace
be born
of your Queen—

Born of the receptive
Mind when it
is one with you,
the expressive;

Born of all the
Myrtles, Marys,
Joans and
Jeannes,

Or whatever is the name
that will give it
birth—

Male or female,

Let there be room
in all

Of the inns of
the earth—

Mine, yours
his and hers—

Black, white
yellow, red, brown
or green!

Let your one and
only son,

Consciousness
be mine,

And everyone's
who breathes
the air

Of your heaven
or who is fired
by your inspiration,

Warmed by your
accomplishment

Or drinks the wine
of your Love,

Which maintains
this order
of things,

This Christmas
and every day
of this
New Year—

And more
to come.

TELL ME

Mind, tell me
more about
yourself,

I am really suffering
to know
more
than

I am conscious
of.

What is your
secret
You are so silent
of?

That I am you
and you are
me?

That I know all
that I am
trying to
find?

And that asking
out there

Will get me
nowhere?

Then speak
and I will
hear,

The things that
lie in
memory

Or let me say
the things of
today

Or of the future
if Mind
knows
all

There is,
or is to be.

Just tell me, Mind
if there is
more
than books
can
tell—

But will as soon
as we know
ourselves
to be

Expressive and receptive,
the all important
Male and
Female

Responsible for all
of creation's
biological
life

And all duration
and everything
in between.

In this universe
they alone
can make

This a place of
friendly
existence

And we can see
truly, how much
depends on
us,

For if we are these two
ourselves,

One with the Father,
One with the Mother;

No longer just the
sons of God;

We have expanded
our consciousness;
past just being part
conscious;
We are that pair
in Love,

And they are us,
who will give
birth to a
new consciousness.

That has been your
secret

That you have made
no secret
of at
all.

PART IV: WITH OPEN ARMS
TO THE FUTURE

WHERE THE FUTURE LIES

All my life has been
past

Up to this very
moment.

All that is ahead
of me
is the
future.

I can look back
and see how
I have
come

But looking ahead
is like a
flat
earth,

All I can see is a
drop off,

But I know it will
not be.

As we found out

The earth proved
to be
round

And round my
future will
be—

I'll only see it
when I get
there,

Except in dreams
and my
imagination.

WHAT DREAMS

What dreams could
I now have
at eighty-eight
years old?

I've painted paintings,
I've written books

And built houses
large and
small.

Would I dream
of being
ninety,

Or how about
four hundred
years old?

Just being is not
enough

Or is it now?

For just in being
without even
thinking
about
it

I am as old as MAN
And as young as the
just born
child.

WHY WORK SO HARD

Why do we work
so hard for
bread and
butter?

Why can't we just
visualize it
on the
platter?

Or who needs
butter
these
days?

Is bread the staff
of life
still?

What will happen
when we have
eaten

All of the fish
in the ocean?

How can we multiply
the loaves
and the
fishes?

How is it that two by two
equals four
and not
five?

What we are getting at
is not reason
but
truth—

Pure mathematics,

That which can't be
tampered with
and get the
right
answer.

I am not just trying
to make a sing-
song
sing,

I am trying to get at
the real
thing,

As a thing is one thing
and not
another,

I am trying to get to
the truth.

Where are the potential
fish—

In the water
or in a basket
or in the Mind?

When a lake is formed
and remains
there,

Surrounded by land
and arched
by sky,

And no man has
been there,

How is it that fish
are found?

What multiplier
will ring up
the truth
but

That, every fraction
is in the
Mind,

And that Mind,
everywhere,

Not just in heads!

Our brains are all
crumpled up
there,

And they are supposed
to remember.

So I'll pick my
brain for
the
truth,

But not by reason,
but with open raised
up arms—

And hard work and
for more than
just bread
and butter,

But because for
curiosity sake.

And this makes all
the difference
in the
world,

Because that is where
the future
lies.

And that is why we
go out there
to see

The fish in the lake—

And praise the Mind
that put them
there

And is itself
the fish

And the bread
elsewhere.

WHAT HAS HAPPENED

Einstein is quoted as saying,
"I want to know the thoughts
of God, the rest are details."

How can we know
the thoughts of God

When our thoughts
are caught up
and snagged
by detail?

How can water
remain water
in the brackish
edges of a
stream?

It is as simple as the
answer to
that.

The thoughts of God
according to
our notion
of God,

Are pure.

So is water, water
everywhere.

We go to great lengths
to keep our drinking
water
pure.

So, with our thoughts
we have to go to
great lengths

And not get bogged
down in the
mire of
depression

Over, "Why did that
son-of-a-bitch
do that or this
to me?

Or why should I
have cancer,

Or rats in my house,

Or not a penny in the
sugar jar
on the
shelf?"

Who was it in the Bible
who was told
to go wash
himself
in the river Jordan?

That is what we need.

We need to wash
ourselves
with the purity of thought;

We can do it when
we take a
shower,

And when we get
on the street
who should
we
meet

But the one-time
son-of-a-bitch,

But now strangely
enough see
him

As the son of
God.

And this will
pick him
up

And send him
cheerfully
on his
way

Without realizing
what has
happened.

We don't need to
lecture or to
preach:

That Mind with
us is the mid-
stream,

Pure and
clean.

We can let it spread
and flood
the shallow
places,

And wash away
the muck
and
debris,

From him
and us.

WHY DO I WRITE LIKE THIS

Why not do a text?

Texts are hard work.

This comes with
ease and assurance,

Straight from the
blue
to me and to
you.

I am like an animal
moved by instinct,
born of trial

And born of
experience,

Made into cell,
bone and
marrow.

I and the animal
are of the
same
stuff;

Of a diversified Mind
that urges us
to be
creative,

True to itself.

And to store in
memory

That which through
eons we
have
learned;

And to spring into
action;

Touched by an
urge;
a necessity

Or a fear
for our
life,

Or to write like
this.

WHAT ARE WE DOING

As there is truth
in mathematics
there is truth
by itself.

The Bible puts it
this way:

"The earth is the Lord's
and the fullness
thereof."

Mind is the possessor
and all that
it possesses

Is what this quote
says to
me.

Or Mind is both Spirit
and the substance—
of Spirit;

The intent
in action

To be or not
to be.

As long as there is
spirit
there
is being.

Spirit is a mental
activity.
As long as it is good
it exists.

When it becomes bad
it destroys
and ceases
to exist.

Then error has no
existence

Any more than
a mathematical
error

Means anything.

THE TRUTH IS

The truth is
we are this Mind
expressing itself
and conceiving
what it expresses.

This is what "the
darkness comprehend
not,"

This is to say
that the Mind itself
is learning of
itself;

Through observing
its own
creation,

And the children
are getting
smarter every
day.

This "comprehending
it not"

Is no longer
admissible;

An expression
is completely lost

If it is not
conceived.

We need that balance
between the
male and female;

Too long has the
Male,

"Our Father which
art in heaven"

Not been understood
as anything more
than a
bachelor,

Who magically
had a child
by a virgin
on earth,

Though it all
makes
sense

When unraveled.

Their child is
consciousness,

Born of the
purity of
Mind

And nothing
else.

This is why prayer
straightens things
out,

And this is the
uncontaminated
truth.

LONG AGO

Long ago things
were told
in simple
parable
form;

Told by adepts,
learned,
for listening
ears

And eyes that
could not
read

Or understand.

Today the scientists
are saying
the same
thing

In a different
language

But the same
thing.

That is why
we should
not throw
these stories
away

But see their
meaning in
poetry,

And marvel on
how truly they
speak the
truth,

To you
and
me
today.

IN THE BEGINNING AND IN
THE ENDING

"In the beginning was the Word
and the Word was with
God
and the Word was
God."

What does that
mean?

It means exactly
what it says.

It means that all
energy is in
the word;

In the intent;
In the command;

Scientists are now
saying,
"All material creation
is structured out
of information
and energy."

There is not information
and energy;
They are one

The whole power
is in the
Word;

That is what makes
the Word,
God.

We have super power
in an emergency
because of the
intent to meet
the emergency,

Which is the key
word.

"I am Alpha and Omega,
the beginning and the
ending, saith
the Lord." Revelation 1:8

If "most of what
we call love

Is just a biological
urge"

Then the biological urge
is love.

Which makes for a more than
friendly
universe.

IN TIME AND SPACE

Until we get over
the idea

That Spiritual life
is one thing

And biological life
is another

We will never live
the life that
we could.

If biology is the
study of life
and of working organisms
in plants and animals

And we don't see ourselves
in this category

It is natural that we
have gone to
another extreme.

And have cut our life in
two—biological
and Spiritual.

It is time for these two
extremes to
come to terms
and become one
view.

Two ideas going
full circle were
bound to
meet,

And give us the fullness
of both in
One—Mind.

This is an explosive
idea—

Another Big Bang!

Will we survive the
shock

Or go the way of the
dinosaurs—

Become completely
extinct

From what we are,
but return again
in the eternal life
chain,

To something more
advanced.

This would satisfy
both the biological
story—

And the Spiritual
idea.

This is still going to
extremes
which could be
true.

But why don't we appreciate
what we have
in the middle
of these TWO?

This would do away
with the idea
of extinction

And all the suffering
that leads up to
it;

By knowing that life
is life regardless of
the form that it
takes,

And realizing that we
need not be afraid
of the change.

Change follows a desire
for change

In the manner in which
it was desired,

So helping one to make
that change is
in order of the
day.

Study biology
and see how the
flower fades and
dies

And blooms again

And listen to the tales
of the Spiritualists.

This is down-to-earth
practicality, and it
is a dream

For the future, in
time and
space.

A WORD TO STED

Sted, I thought, at times,
you were mentally
cruel to me.

But you were exactly
what I asked
for—

A man of the world!

It wasn't easy to
be pounded and
welded

Into giving birth to
what I comprehend
now.

I give you full
credit for taxing
my brain.

In loving me you
gave of your
solidity of mind

Which tore down any
remaining other-wordly
views.

Leaving your male
intellect sometimes
frightened—

At what you had
set off in my
mind.

There is not
an other-world;
in this sense.

This is it—
One of Spirit
(the non-stuff of all
stuff as the scientists put it).

It took an urge to
set it all
off

And it takes an urge
to keep it
moving
on

Through The
Way Things Are
Or
Could
Be

No matter
how separate
or different
we are,

No matter
how many times
our two-getherness
is cut off

Each separate part
is a hologram,
a twoness of
One Mind

An house not made
with hands, eternal
in the heavens.
II Corinthians 5:1

Love you still

Myrtle

WHAT BUT THE MIND

Could be that non-stuff
of all stuff?

What could be everywhere
—everybody's Mind,
universally effective—

Without ever our being
aware of it,

We can not see it,
we can not hear it,

But we see and hear
its effect
and call that
reality;

Which only the Mind
can do.

So doing is the essence.

What prompts the doing
and what sustains
it but a love of
doing?

Could we extinguish
ourselves in the
doing—

As so much seems
evident today?

How can you extinguish
anything but an
effect?

You can not touch
the Mind.

In its Love it
Fathers and Mothers
everything.

Then seemingly leaves
us and everything
on our, or its own.

But not so.

We are the same
non-stuff
of all stuff

Potentially the potential
for the furtherance
of the stuff we
call life,

The consciousness of having
a Mind.